bharat babies™

Super Satya Saves the Day

Library of Congress Control Number: 2018908412

CPSIA Code: PRT0818A
ISBN-13: 978-1-64307-117-6

Printed in the United States

RAAKHEE:

For Satya Devi, Athena, and Zahra, the lights of my life.
And for all the children battling pediatric cancer - including Briana,
Addie, and Eli - the bravest superheroes the world has ever seen.

TIM:

To Michael, who nudges me along when I'm not feeling very "super."
And to Satya, my new friend and muse.

SUPER SATYA
SAVES THE DAY

STORY BY
RAAKHEE MIRCHANDANI

PICTURES BY
TIM PALIN

bharat babies™

"HEY!"

SQUEAK SQUEAK SQUEAK

HONK HONNNNN

BEEP BEEP

It was a loud day, on a loud street, in the very loud town of Hoboken.

The fire trucks made fire truck noises, the police cars made police car noises, and the swings at Church Square Park were extra squeaky.

And the knot in Super Satya's stomach felt super tight.

How was she supposed to do all the things that superheroes do if her superhero cape was stuck at the dry cleaner?

Satya wished they could've picked the cape up on the way to school, but the dry cleaner was closed.

Super Mama said she was super late to work and they couldn't wait for the store to open.

They did stop for coffee, though. They always stopped for coffee.
Mama says if she doesn't have any coffee, her head will explode.

ITTLE CITY
BOOKS

100

KWIK
KLEEN

CLOSED

FIRST
NATIO
BANK

Today is going to be the worst, Super Satya thought as they headed to school. All of her superhero powers were in the cape that Super Mama made for her.

And there was just no way her super senses were going to work without it.

At school, Ms. Corinna was teaching the class about communities.

Satya was excited to build her own city, but she couldn't get the structures quite right.

She knew it was because she always did her best
thinking with her cape on her back.

Satya slumped in her chair. Nothing was going right today.
That's when she spotted Tanya, her friend Jahan's lost T-Rex.
Tanya had been missing for days and Jahan had been so super sad.

Super Satya scooped Tanya up and ran over to Jahan, who hugged his pal Satya so tight, she felt some super breath leave her belly.

"Super Satya, you did it! You found her! You really are a hero," Jahan said.

Not without a cape, Satya thought as the class headed out for an afternoon walk.

TWEET
TWEET
TWEET

BLOOT
BLOOOOT
TOOT
TOOT

CHIRP
CHIRP

Outside, the boats were making
boat noises and the birds
were making bird noises.

IT WAS VERY
LOUD.

Suddenly, Super Satya heard a sound that didn't belong. It was
a gentle whimper coming from somewhere near the grass.

As she got closer, the noise got louder. A scared set of puppy eyes peeked out from behind the trash can. "Don't worry little friend, we'll find your family," Super Satya whispered.

In the distance, a boy was holding a leash, running and shouting: "Leo! Leo! Come here, buddy." He looked just as scared as the dog.

"I think he's over here," Super Satya called to the boy.
"He looks really scared and I heard him crying."

TOOT
TOOT

"His collar is too big for him," said the boy. "Thank you for finding him I love him so much and I was really worried! You must have some super hearing to have heard his little cry with all this noise out here!"

Super Satya walked a little straighter on the way back to school.

Her super eyes and ears seemed to work just fine without the cape.

After school, Satya was missing her cape more than ever. Today was the day she had planned to conquer the tallest slide in Hoboken, but there was **no way** that was happening without her trusty cape.

"FORGET IT."

But then, Super Satya started thinking about the day.

She thought about all the super things she had done and all the friends she had helped.

With a quick nod and wink to her Super Dada, Super Satya ran up the steps and took her spot at the top of the slide.

WOOOSSHHH WOOOSSHHH

HONK HONNNNK

CHIRP CHIRP

She was scared, but she was also super excited.

Without thinking about anything else, she let go.

"You did it!" Super Dada exclaimed as he picked her up and gave her a kiss. "You are super brave!"

On the way home, Super Dada and Super Satya stopped at the dry cleaner - just like Super Mama said they would.

The cape was pressed and ready.

"Thanks, Mrs. Markowitz! You always take such good care of my cape," Satya said as she left the shop.

Having her cape back sure felt great, Satya thought, as she draped it over her shoulders. But she knew her day was super because she was . . .